Tadpole Books are published by Jump!, 5357 Penn Avenue South, Minneapolis, MN 55419, www.jumplibrary.com

Copyright ©2019 Jump. International copyright reserved in all countries. No part of this book may be reproduced in any form without written permission from the publisher.

Editor: Jenna Trnka **Designer:** Anna Peterson **Translator:** Annette Granat

Photo Credits: Lepas/Shutterstock, cover; chengyuzheng/iStock, 1; inhauscreative/iStock, 2-3, 16tm; Lindaparton/Dreamstime, 4-5, 16tr; stanley45/iStock, 6-7, 16br; Volodymyr_Plysiuk/iStock, 8-9, 16bm; Somsak Sudthangtum/123rf, 10-11, 16tl; Oleksandr Lytvynenko/Shutterstock, 12-13, 16bl; Juniors Bildarchiv/Alamy, 14-15.

Library of Congress Cataloging-in-Publication Data is available at www.loc.gov or upon request from the publisher.
978-1-64128-088-4 (hardcover)
978-1-64128-089-1 (ebook)

LOS BEBÉS DEL BOSQUE

LOS GAZAPOS

por Genevieve Nilsen

TABLA DE CONTENIDO

Los gazapos 2

Repaso de palabras 16

Índice 16

LOS GAZAPOS

Veo gazapos.

Son conejos bebés.

Nacen en un nido.

nido

El nido está en el bosque.

Se esconden.

Comen pasto.

Les crecen colas blancas.

Les crecen orejas altas.

¡Corren rápido!

REPASO DE PALABRAS

colas

gazapos

nido

orejas

pasto

se esconden

ÍNDICE

bosque 5
colas 11
comen 9
corren 15
gazapos 2
nido 4, 5
orejas 13
se esconden 7